To my parents for teaching me the way,

To my wife for walking this path with me in love,

To my children for showing us all wonder and joy,

To my grandmother for teaching that a penny
is more than just a coin.

www.mascotbooks.com

Oh, the Places You've Been

For more information, please contact:
Mascot Books
620 Herndon Parkway #320
Herndon, VA 20170
info@mascotbooks.com

Library of Congress Control Number: 2019904760

CPSIA Code: PRT1119A
ISBN-13: 978-1-64307-266-1

Printed in the United States

OH, THE places You've BEEN

Written by Ben Everard with Mary Everard

Illustrated by Andrea Alemanno

Once upon a midsummer's day
lived a penny who wanted to play.
Staring at the sky so wide,
he pondered quietly on his side.

It just so happened right there and then,
down the street sprinted Harper Glen.
A feisty girl of no more than eight
who was running just a little bit late.

Something caught her eye as she passed—
an old copper penny in the sun that flashed.

The penny was old, dirty, and dark.
Lost of all shine, all shimmer, all spark.
Should she keep it? Should she toss it aside?
In spite of its looks, there was something inside
that made Harper say,
this penny can stay.

And that's when she heard
a faint whisper of words.

"I'm not much to look at, this is quite clear,
but I have wondrous adventures both far and near."

"I've been high and I've been low.
I've been fast and I've been slow.
I've been hot and I've been cold.
I've been scared and I've been bold.

I've been found and then lost,
dropped and then tossed,
over and over and over again.
But oh the places I have been!"

"This chip you see on my coppery face
is a mark that I completely embrace.
From my time underwater, chilly and wet,
but then saved by a fisherman's net."

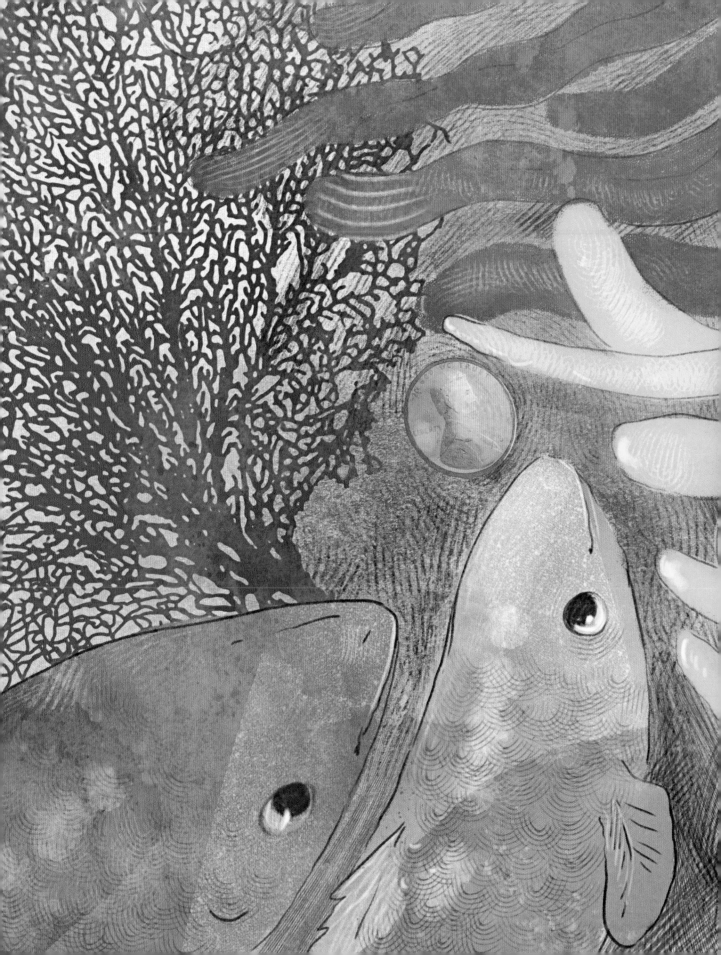

"A forest of redwoods is next on my list—
towering trees overclouded with mist.
Here I embraced solitude and defiance
and discovered the power of nature and science."

"Once I was completely buried in snow!
Strong winds from afar would constantly blow.

It was rugged and rough on top of that mountain.
How I longed for the days when I'd lounge in a fountain.
As I shivered on that summit, wondering how to escape
a frozen embrace as my ultimate fate,

I kept my wits and my grit and remembered this trick:
When you're knocked to the ground, get back up really quick."

"A city with buildings as high as the sky"

"A field full of fireflies who won't say goodbye."

"A hillside near waves crashing under the moon."

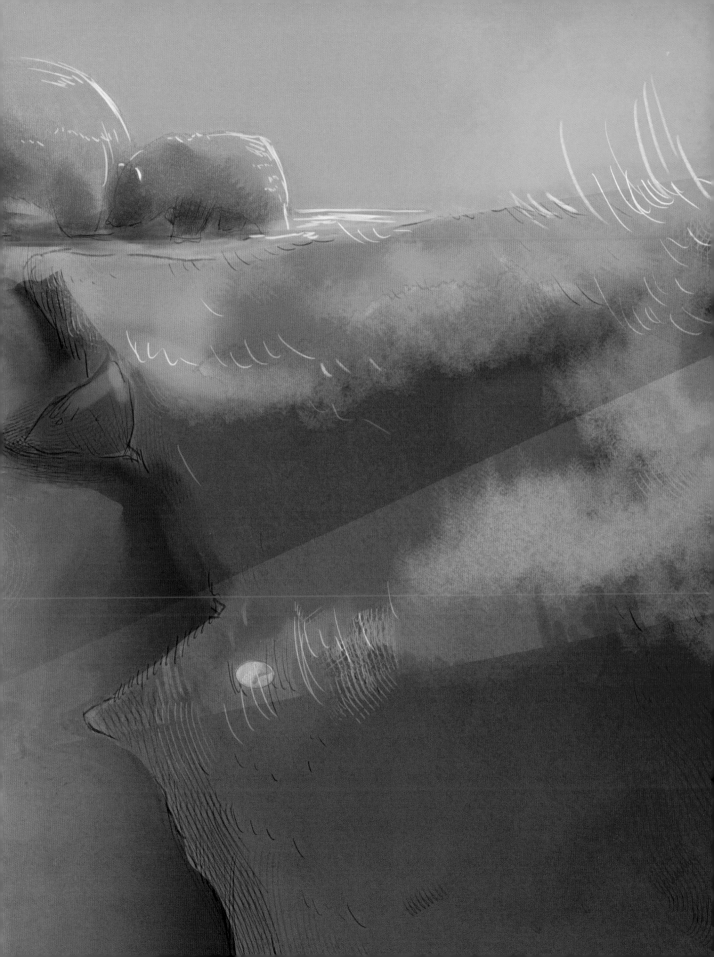

"A river with rocks that were smoother than smooth.

All of these places are places I've moved,
far beyond this sidewalk's groove."

"Back in the year 1969
I was recently minted and had all my shine.
I went for a ride way up in the sky,
bound for the moon, higher than high.

I was nervous as could be floating up in a rocket,
but when Neil stepped out I smiled from his pocket.
We were as far as far can go, past the sky and on the moon.
Maybe one day, Harper Glen, you will go there too."

"There's advice to be learned from the tales I've told.
Even pennies long forgotten have adventures to behold.

Sometimes it's the oldest and frailest of things
with the greatest of stories their full life brings.

Next time you see a penny alone on its side,
ponder for a moment as you break your stride.
Think of all the wonders that penny may have seen
and ask a simple question ..."

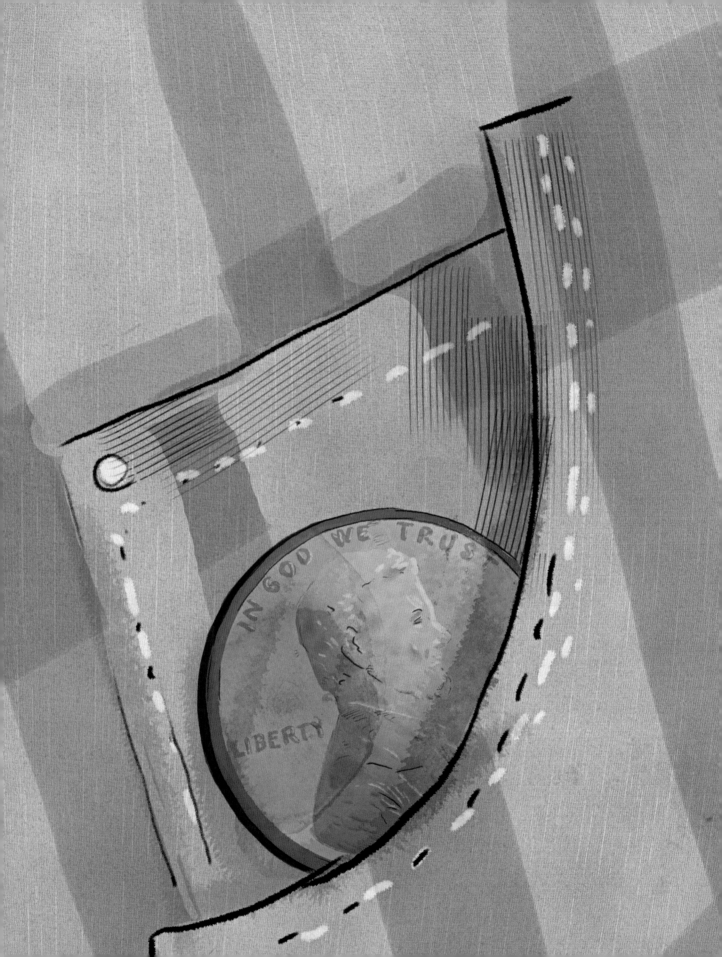

where HAS your PENNY BEEN?

ABOUT THE *author*

A husband, father, lawyer, writer, and film producer,
Ben Everard lives in Los Angeles, California,
by way of Crystal Lake, Illinois.